Bangers and Cash

Written by Tom Easton
Illustrated by Matt Buckingham

WAYLAND

Captain Flint was dancing a jig on the deck of the Stuck Pig.

"This is the biggest haul we've had this year!" he cried in delight.

The Poor Pirates gathered round to admire the treasure that they'd just captured from a French ship.

"This is the **only** haul we've had this year," Arthur Sandwich pointed out.

"What shall we spend the money on?"
asked Selma, the first mate.

"Fancy clothes," said the Captain, "and
a brand new desk for my cabin."

"I need some new glasses," Big Ben called down from the crow's nest.

"Well, I'm hungry. I want to eat!" said Arthur, eyeing an enormous sack of sausages they'd stolen from the French ship's galley.

"First things first," the Captain said.
"The ship is covered with barnacles.
We'll need to go into port to scrape
them off."

All the pirates groaned.
Barnacle-scraping was the
worst job on the Seven Seas.

"Don't worry," the Captain grinned.
"Now we have all this treasure, we can
eat sausages while we pay someone else
to do the work!"

"Hurray!" cried the Poor Pirates.

The pirates pulled up the anchor and began to sail towards land.

Suddenly the ship shuddered to a stop, throwing the pirates forwards. They landed in a heap next to the mast.

"What was that?" the Captain yelled.

11

Selma peered over the side. The ship had hit a sandbank. The Stuck Pig was stuck fast!

"It's all right," said Selma. "If we make the ship lighter, we'll float off again."

"How can we do that?" Arthur asked.

"I've had a **brilliant** idea," said Captain Flint, a clever gleam in his eye.

It turned out that the Captain's idea wasn't so brilliant!

"Urgh, I feel sick," Big Ben said.

"Me, too. I'm never eating sausages again!" groaned Pegleg Pete.

"Mmmm. I love sausages! But Captain, eating all these sausages won't really make the ship lighter, will it?" said Arthur, trying not to burp. "We haven't got rid of them. We've just moved them from the sack into our tummies."

"Why didn't you say this before?"
the Captain roared.

"I was hungry," whimpered Arthur.

"It's the treasure chest weighing us down, not the sausages," squawked Long John's Parrot.

"I know what to do," said Pegleg Pete. "Let's take the treasure out of the chest and divide it up between us."

"That might work," agreed the Captain.

The pirates spent the next hour arguing about who got what treasure. Somehow the Captain ended up with most of it but, at last, the chest was empty.

But the Stuck Pig was still stuck fast.

"It must be the same problem as
before, Captain," said Arthur. "We're not
taking the treasure off the ship. We're
just moving it from the chest into
our pockets."

"OK," said the Captain. "I know! Let's launch the jolly boat and the chest can float in that while we tow it behind."

So the pirates put all the treasure back
into the chest. Then they launched
the jolly boat and began lowering the
treasure chest into it.

But the chest was just too heavy! With
a gurgle and a glug, the jolly boat and
all the treasure slowly sank to the
bottom of the ocean.

"Oops," whispered Selma. "That wasn't supposed to happen, was it?"

"No, it wasn't," shouted the Captain, his face bulging with anger. "You useless pirates have just lost me my treasure. For that you can clean the barnacles off this ship yourselves. I don't care how long it takes you!"

Captain Flint stormed into his cabin,
slamming the door behind him.

The Poor Pirates miserably steered the
boat into port and began scraping off
the barnacles.

"I hate barnacles," Selma said, as a
very large one hit her on the nose.
"And I still feel sick from eating all
those sausages."

"Me, too," Big Ben replied. "I do
hope it's not sausages for tea tonight."

"Hold on. Where's Arthur?" asked Pegleg Pete, looking around.

Sure enough, Arthur was nowhere to be seen.

When the pirates had finished
barnacle-scraping, they collapsed onto
the deck. At that moment, Arthur
arrived back on board the ship.

"Where have you been?" growled the Captain, as Arthur dragged a large sack behind him.

"Well," admitted Arthur, "I found a gold coin that had fallen into my pocket. So I went into town to get us something to cheer us all up!"

"What did you get? Is it fancy clothes?" the Captain asked, eagerly.

"New glasses?" Big Ben suggested.

"No," Arthur replied. "Something even better!"

And he opened the sack to reveal...

...more sausages!

"Oh, no!" the Poor Pirates cried.

They all rushed to the side of the
Stuck Pig and were very sick indeed!

START READING is a series of highly enjoyable books for beginner readers. **The books have been carefully graded to match the Book Bands widely used in schools.** This enables readers to be sure they choose books that match their own reading ability.

Look out for the Band colour on the book in our Start Reading logo.

The Bands are:

| Pink Band 1A & 1B |
| Red Band 2 |
| Yellow Band 3 |
| Blue Band 4 |
| Green Band 5 |
| Orange Band 6 |
| Turquoise Band 7 |
| Purple Band 8 |
| Gold Band 9 |

START READING books can be read independently or shared with an adult. They promote the enjoyment of reading through satisfying stories, plays and non-fiction narratives, which are supported by fun illustrations and photographs.

Tom Easton lives in Surrey, works in London and spends a lot of time travelling between the two, which is when he does his writing. Tom has written books for children, teenagers and adults, under a variety of pseudonyms. He has three children and is looking forward to having macaroni cheese tonight.

Matt Buckingham would have rather liked a job as a pirate if he hadn't become an illustrator. The only problem is Matt gets seasick, so it's probably best if he sticks to drawing pirates instead.

Bangers and Cash

First published in 2011
by Wayland

Text copyright © Tom Easton
Illustration copyright © Matt Buckingham

Wayland
338 Euston Road
London NW1 3BH

Wayland Australia
Level 17/207 Kent Street
Sydney, NSW 2000

Series Editor: Louise John
Editor: Katie Woolley
Cover design: Paul Cherrill
Design: D.R.ink
Consultant: Shirley Bickler

A CIP catalogue record for this book is available from the British Library.

ISBN 9780750264938

Printed in China

Wayland is a division of Hachette Children's Books,
an Hachette UK Company

www.hachette.co.uk